READING

RECOVERY

Be Ready at Eight

Be Ready at Eight

By Peggy Parish
Illustrated by Cynthia Fisher

Ready-to-Read
Simon & Schuster Books for Young Readers

Simon & Schuster Books for Young Readers
An imprint of Simon & Schuster Children's Publishing Division
1230 Avenue of the Americas
New York, NY 10020

The text for this book was set in 17 point Utopia.
The illustrations were rendered in watercolor and ink.

Printed and bound in the United States of America

10 9 8 7 6 5 4 3 2 1

The Library of Congress has cataloged the Simon & Schuster Books for
Young Readers Edition as follows:

Parish, Peggy.
Be ready at eight / by Peggy Parish ; illustrated by Cynthia Fisher.
p.   cm.—(Ready-to-Read)
Summary: Absent-minded Miss Molly tries to remember why she tied a
string around her finger—and why all her friends plan to see her at eight.
[I. Memory—Fiction. 2. Birthdays—Fiction.] I. Fisher, Cynthia, ill.
II. Title. III. Series.
PZ7.P219Bc 1996 [E]—dc20 96-3709
ISBN 0-689-80792-9 (hc) 0-689-80791-0 (pbk.)

To my mother, Gram Sumner,
and all the Miss Mollys I've known
—C. F.

Miss Molly woke up.
She looked at the clock.
"Nine o'clock!" she said.
"My, I slept late."
Miss Molly stretched.
Something caught her eye.

"Oh," she said.
"A string around my finger.
That's to remind me.
Something special
is happening today.
Now what could it be?"

Miss Molly got out of bed.
She touched her toes ten times.
"I did my exercises," she said.
"But that's not special.
I do them every day."

Miss Molly went into
the bathroom.
She brushed her teeth.
She washed her face.
She combed her hair.
"That's done," she said.
"But I do that every day.
That's not special."
Miss Molly got dressed.
"I never was good at
remembering," she said.

9

She shook her head.
"My mother would get
so mad at me.
She sent me to the store for peas.
I came home with carrots,"
said Miss Molly.

"She told me to take
the baby to the park.
I forgot to bring her home.
My father said
I would outgrow it.
I would learn to remember.
And maybe I will."
Miss Molly laughed.

"But it's more fun this way.
Every day is full of surprises
and puzzles," she said.
She looked at her finger.
"That's my puzzle for today."
Miss Molly cooked her breakfast.
She ate it and she thought.
"Now, what must I remember?"
she said.
"What is happening today?"
She thought some more.

"I'll look at the calendar!"
said Miss Molly.
"Maybe I wrote myself a note."
She went to the calendar.
"Oh, dear," she said.
"There are lots of notes.
But I forget the date."

Miss Molly thought
some more.
"The newspaper!"
she said.
"That will give me
the date."
Miss Molly went to
the porch.
She picked up the
paper.
"Thursday, the
twenty-third,"
she read.

Miss Molly looked at the calendar.
"Here it is," she said.
"Here is a note that says,
'Be ready at eight.'
Be ready for what?" she said.

She shook her head.
"I just don't know," she said.
"I'll do my housework.
Then I'll try to find out."

She hustled and she bustled.
Soon her work was done.
"Now I'll take a walk," she said.
"I must find out
what is special today.
I must know why
I have to be ready at eight."

Miss Molly got her bag.
She started her walk.
She saw Mr. Block cutting roses.
"The flower show!" said Miss Molly.

"That is special.

It must be today."
She walked to the fence.
"Mr. Block," she called.
"Are those roses
for the flower show?"

19

Mr. Block looked puzzled.

"The flower show?" he said.

"That was last month."

"That's right," said Miss Molly.

"I was there.

I do love flower shows."

Mr. Block said,

"These roses are for–"

Miss Molly waited

for him to say more.

"They are for something

very special," said Mr. Block.

"Oh," said Miss Molly.
She walked on.
"I wish he had told me
what was special," she said.
"I couldn't ask.

That wouldn't have been nice."

She came to the church.
Two women were going in.
Each was carrying a dish.
"The church supper!" said Miss Molly.
"Maybe it's tonight."
She walked into the church.

"Good morning, Miss Molly,"
said Dr. Wade. "Can I help you?"
"I wanted to ask
about the church supper,"
said Miss Molly.

"Oh, yes," said Dr. Wade.
"That is next month.
We hope you will help."
"Indeed I will," said Miss Molly.
"I do love church suppers.
They are very special."
"And this is a very special
day for you," said Dr. Wade.
"Oh, yes," said Miss Molly.

She left the church.
"What did he mean?" she said.
"I know it's a special day.
But I don't know why!"

Miss Molly saw Mrs. Miller.
She had her pet skunk,
Muffin, with her.
"The pet show!" said Miss Molly.
"Maybe I'm giving the prizes."

Mrs. Miller came closer.
"How pretty Muffin looks,"
said Miss Molly. "I hope
she wins a prize tonight."
Mrs. Miller looked puzzled.
"Are pets invited tonight?"
she said.
Then Miss Molly looked puzzled.
"Isn't the pet show tonight?"
she said.
Mrs. Miller smiled and said,
"That's next Thursday night."
"I'll be there," said Miss Molly.
"I do love pet shows."

"But I'll see you tonight
at eight," said Mrs. Miller.
She and Muffin walked away.

Miss Molly stood there.
"See me where?" she said.
Then she walked on.
She came to the post office.
"I'll buy some stamps,"
she said.
"I always need them."

"Good morning," said the clerk.
"A book of stamps, please,"
said Miss Molly.
"Are you writing more letters?"
he said.
"You mailed a lot last week."
Miss Molly said nothing.
She paid for the stamps.
Then Miss Molly went home.

"I wrote letters last week?"
she said.
Then she laughed and said,
"Maybe I finally paid my bills.
I do forget to do that."
Miss Molly ate her lunch.
She looked at the string.

Miss Molly shook her head.
"I must think harder," she said.
"Sometimes rocking helps."
She went to her front porch.
She sat down and rocked.

Miss Molly looked
across the street.
She saw Jane and her mother.
Jane was carrying
her dancing slippers.

"The dancing school show!"
said Miss Molly. "That's it!"
She called, "Is the show
at eight tonight, Jane?"
"No," said Jane.
"Today is just a lesson."

Jane's mother said,
"The show is next week.
We will take you."
"Good," said Miss Molly.
"I do love dance shows."
Jane said, "After my lesson,
we're going to–"
"Hush, Jane," said her mother.
"That's a secret.

We'll see you tonight,
Miss Molly."
"Everybody is going to see me
tonight," said Miss Molly.
"But where are they
going to see me?"

She saw Tommy coming. He had
his baseball and bat.
"The ball game!" said Miss Molly.
"The games are always at eight.
Everybody goes to them. Everybody
will see me there. That must be it."
"Hi, Miss Molly," said Tommy.
"I'll be at the game tonight,"
said Miss Molly. "But Miss Molly,"
said Tommy, "this is Thursday.
Our games are always on Fridays."

"That's right," said Miss Molly.
"I'll be there tomorrow night.
I do love ball games."
"But I'll see you tonight,"
said Tommy.
"I found something really–"
Tommy stopped.

Then he said, "Oops, I almost told."
Tommy ran down the street.
"So much is going to happen
on other nights," said Miss Molly.
"But I want to know about
eight o'clock tonight.
Everybody else seems to know."

Miss Molly went inside.

"I'll have a cup of tea," she said.

She started to the kitchen.

The back doorbell rang.

"Who could that be?" she said.

Miss Molly called, "Come in."

A boy came in.

"Here are the sodas
you ordered," he said.
"Sodas?" said Miss Molly.
"When did I order sodas?"
"Last week," said the boy.
"You said to bring them today."
"Oh," said Miss Molly.
"Thank you."

Miss Molly looked at
the cans of soda.
"I declare," she said.
"Why did I do that?"
She thought a while.
"I mailed lots of letters.
I ordered lots of soda.
Everybody is going to see
me tonight," she said.
Miss Molly laughed.
She clapped her hands.
"I know!" she said.

"I'm giving a party.
I do love parties."

Miss Molly stopped.
"But why am I giving a party?
Let me think.
Is somebody moving away?
Is somebody getting married?
Is somebody having a birthday?
Is somebody having a baby?"

Miss Molly shook her head.
"Well, it doesn't matter,"
she said. "A party means a cake.
I must get busy."
And Miss Molly did.

Soon she had her cake baked.

Miss Molly looked at it.

"Since it's a party cake,

I'll make it fancy," she said.

"I do love fancy cakes."

Miss Molly worked and worked.

"There," she said.

"That is pretty."

She looked at the string
on her finger.
Miss Molly laughed.
"I give up," she said.
"I know one part of my puzzle.
But the other part
will have to surprise me.

I'll be ready at eight
and see what happens."
Miss Molly yawned.
"I'm tired," she said.
"I'll just take a little rest."
Miss Molly lay down.
Soon she was fast asleep.

Later she woke up.
She looked up at the
clock.

"Oh," she said.
"I must hurry."
Miss Molly ate her
supper.

She took her bath.
She used her nicest
bath powder.

She put on her
best dress.

Then Miss Molly sat down.

"I'm so excited," she said.

"I do love surprises."

The clock began to strike.
Bong, bong, bong, bong,
bong, bong, bong, bong.

And the doorbell rang.

Miss Molly hurried to the door.

She opened it.

Her porch was filled with people.
"HAPPY BIRTHDAY!" they shouted.

Miss Molly threw up her hands.
"So that's it!" she said.

Everybody laughed.
Miss Molly laughed, too.
"Come in, come in," she said.
"I'll be right with you."

Miss Molly hurried to the kitchen.
Quickly she added
some things to the cake.
She picked it up.
Miss Molly went back
to her friends.

Miss Molly began to sing,
"Happy birthday to me,
Happy birthday to me."
She put the cake down.
"Now," she said, "I can
take off this string."
"Oh, Molly," said her sister.
"You forgot again."
"I sure did," said Miss Molly.
"I gave myself a surprise party."
Then she laughed and said,
"And I was really surprised."

Everybody shouted,
"That's our Miss Molly!"
Tommy lit the candles.
And everybody sang
"Happy Birthday."

The End